PINKERTON, BEHAVE!

STEVEN KELLOGG

PUFFIN BOOKS

PUFFIN BOOKS
Published by the Penguin Group
Penguin Putnam Books for Young Readers, 345 Hudson Street, New York, New York 10014, U.S.A.
Penguin Books Ltd, 80 Strand, London WC2R ORL, England
Penguin Books Australia Ltd, Ringwood, Victoria, Australia
Penguin Books Canada Ltd, 10 Alcorn Avenue, Toronto, Ontario, Canada M4V 3B2
Penguin Books (N.Z.) Ltd, 182-190 Wairau Road, Auckland 10, New Zealand

Penguin Books Ltd, Registered Offices: Harmondsworth, Middlesex, England

First published in the United States of America by
Dial Books for Young Readers, a division of Penguin Books USA Inc., 1979
Published by Puffin Books, a division of Penguin Putnam Books for Young Readers, 2002

1 3 5 7 9 10 8 6 4 2

THE LIBRARY OF CONGRESS HAS CATALOGED THE DIAL EDITION AS FOLLOWS:
Kellogg, Steven
Pinkerton, Behave!
Summary/ His behavior may be rather unconventional, but Pinkerton, the dog, proves it doesn't really matter.
[1. Dogs—Fiction] I. Title.
PZ7.K292Pi [E] 78-31794
ISBN 0-8037-6573-8/ISBN 0-8037-6575-4/(lib. bdg.)

Puffin Books ISBN 0-14-230007-1

Printed in Hong Kong

For Helen,
my best friend and
the person who chose
the Great Pinkerton

Every new puppy has to learn to behave.
First I'll teach Pinkerton to come when he's called.

Come!

He can learn to bring us the newspaper.

Fetch!

From now on *I'll* fetch the newspaper.

But it's important for him to defend the house if a burglar comes.

We'll pretend this dummy is a burglar.

Get the burglar, Pinkerton!

I think we need some professional help.
Pinkerton will have to go to obedience school.

When this poor creature sees how well the other dogs behave, he will understand what we expect of him.

We begin with a simple command. Come.

COME! COME! COME!

We cannot hold back the entire class for one confused student.
On to the next lesson!

Every dog must fetch the evening paper.

Fetch, you fleabrain, FETCH!

Our next lesson is a most important one.
Get the burglar!

Pinkerton sets a poor example for the rest of the class.
Unless he shows some improvement, he will be dismissed.

We will now review all that we have learned.
Dogs! Pay attention!

COME!

FETCH!

GET THE BURGLAR!

OUT! OUT! OUT! OUT!

Mom, you and Pinkerton look pretty tired.
Why don't you go to bed and get a good night's rest?

Pleasant dreams, Pinkerton.

This is a stickup, lady. Don't move, or I'll blast you and your silly hound to chicken powder.

Pssssssst! Pinkerton! A burglar!

I warned you, lady.

Pinkerton! Fetch!

GRRRRRRRRRR

Pinkerton! Come!

Pinkerton, I'm a burglar.

I love you, Pinkerton.